Enid Blyton™

TOY TOWN STORIES

MR PLOD'S SEARCH FOR NODDY

S L M

First published in Great Britain by HarperCollins Publishers Ltd in 1997

3 5 7 9 10 8 6 4

ISBN: 0 00 172009 0

Story by Fiona Cummings
Cover design and illustrations by County Studios
A CIP catalogue for this title is available from the British Library.

Printed and bound in Singapore

Enid Blyton™

TOY TOWN STORIES

MR PLOD'S SEARCH FOR NODDY

Collins

An Imprint of HarperCollins*Publishers*

"Ah, five o'clock at last," Mr Plod said, glancing at his watch. "That means it is time to go to Noddy's for tea. How kind of him to invite me!"

Mr Plod whistled as he plodded his way towards Noddy's house. He was really looking forward to the tea. He had been so busy at the police station.

Mr Plod soon reached Noddy's house.
He knocked on Noddy's front door.

There was no answer.

"That's odd," Mr Plod mumbled to himself. "Very odd indeed!"

Mr Plod tried the door and found that it was open. "How strange!" he thought.

It seemed even stranger when he saw a chair lying on its side in Noddy's house. Noddy was normally so tidy.

"There's something fishy going on here," Mr Plod said. "I don't like it one little bit. Ah, look – I was right!"

He had suddenly spotted a note lying on Noddy's table. It read:

If you want me to bring him back, it will cost two sixpences.

Mr Plod immediately put his whistle to his mouth and blew hard three times.

Perhaps a wicked person had dragged Noddy away from his house and was asking for money to set him free.

Mr Plod suddenly leapt behind the door. He could hear someone coming. It must be that wicked person coming to collect his money!

"Ah-ha! Got you!" Mr Plod cried, as the person stepped through the door. It was Bert Monkey!

“Let me go, let me go!” Bert Monkey wailed, trying to wriggle free.

“No, it’s jail for you,” Mr Plod said. “Unless you tell me at once where you have put Noddy.”

Bert Monkey WRIGGLED and WRIGGLED but still he could not break free.

"I haven't put Noddy anywhere," he pleaded.

Mr Plod snorted. "Haven't you indeed?" he said. "Then why have you come to his house? To collect the two sixpences – that's why!"

Bert Monkey really did not know what Mr Plod was talking about. "What two sixpences?" he asked. "I only came to Noddy's house because I heard your police whistle!"

And at that Bert Monkey suddenly wrapped his tail around Mr Plod's leg and YANKED very hard. Mr Plod fell to the floor!

Bert Monkey ran off, very annoyed indeed. All he had been doing was trying to help the silly policeman!

Mr Plod rubbed himself as he got up from the floor. His face was very red. What a stupid mistake he had made!

Suddenly, Mr Plod heard someone else coming towards the door. Ah, so *this* was the wicked person who had dragged Noddy away!

This time Mr Plod hid under the table. He peeped out from under the table cloth. Who *was* the person?

It was Sammy Sailor!

Mr Plod kept very quiet as Sammy Sailor walked over to the table. Then Mr Plod suddenly JUMPED OUT!

"It's a bad day for you, my lad!" Mr Plod cried, putting a handcuff on Sammy's wrist. "Tell me where Noddy is or you'll go straight to jail!"

"Come on, my lad, I want answers!" Mr Plod demanded. He sounded so fierce that it made Sammy shiver. "Where have you taken Noddy?"

It was then that Sammy remembered a special trick that an old sailor had taught him. He suddenly twisted his wrist and gave his hand a sharp tug. It slipped right out of the handcuff!

Then Sammy quickly snapped the handcuff on to the table leg. CLICK! Poor Mr Plod could not move.

“I haven’t taken Noddy anywhere,” Sammy cried, as he ran for the door. “It was Noddy who was meant to be taking *me* – to the harbour! My brother’s ship is arriving soon.”

Again Mr Plod went very red. And he stayed red for quite a while. Then he heard someone else coming towards the door. Who was it this time?

It was NODDY!

"Mr Plod!" Noddy cried. "I've been waiting for you at your police station. You had invited me there for tea."

Mr Plod went even redder than he had the last two times. So Noddy had not been taken from his house after all!

Noddy laughed and laughed when Mr Plod told him what he thought had happened. Noddy explained that *he* had written the note on the table – for Sammy Sailor.

"If I had driven Sammy *to* the harbour," said Noddy, "I would have been late for our tea. But I was able to drive Sammy and his brother *back* from the harbour. As long as they paid me two sixpences!"

Noddy explained that he had left his front door open so Sammy would find the note he had left for him. As for the chair – Noddy had knocked it over himself. He had been a bit late for their tea and was in a hurry!

Still chuckling, Noddy took the key from Mr Plod's back pocket so he could unlock the handcuffs. He asked Mr Plod if he would write down what had happened in his notebook.

"Oh no," Mr Plod laughed, "all I am going to write down is where our *next* tea will be. If I had written it down *this* time, perhaps I wouldn't have made such a mistake!"

THE NODDY CLASSIC LIBRARY
by Enid Blyton™

1. NODDY GOES TO TOYLAND
2. HURRAH FOR LITTLE NODDY
3. NODDY AND HIS CAR
4. HERE COMES NODDY AGAIN!
5. WELL DONE NODDY!
6. NODDY GOES TO SCHOOL
7. NODDY AT THE SEASIDE
8. NODDY GETS INTO TROUBLE
9. NODDY AND THE MAGIC RULER
10. YOU FUNNY LITTLE NODDY
11. NODDY MEETS FATHER CHRISTMAS
12. NODDY AND TESSIE BEAR
13. BE BRAVE LITTLE NODDY!
14. NODDY AND THE BUMPY-DOG
15. DO LOOK OUT NODDY!
16. YOU'RE A GOOD FRIEND NODDY!
17. NODDY HAS AN ADVENTURE
18. NODDY GOES TO SEA
19. NODDY AND THE BUNKEY
20. CHEER UP LITTLE NODDY!
21. NODDY GOES TO THE FAIR
22. MR PLOD AND LITTLE NODDY
23. NODDY AND THE TOOTLES
24. NODDY AND THE AEROPLANE

Available in hardback
Published by HarperCollins